THE CHRISTMAS DONKEY

BY *Donna Thornton*

ILLUSTRATIONS BY *Lynne Pryor*

The Christmas Donkey

©2011 Donna Thornton

Illustrated by Lynne Ballenger Pryor

Edited by Kacie Dalton

Printed in China

ISBN: 978-1-93550-773-4

eISBN: 978-1-62020-084-1

Unless otherwise stated, all Scripture quotations are from THE HOLY BIBLE, NEW INTERNATIONAL VERSION®, NIV® Copyright © 1973, 1978, 1984, 2010 by Biblica, Inc.™ Used by permission. All rights reserved worldwide.

Cover Design & Page Layout by Dena Hynes Design: *www.creativedena.com*

AMBASSADOR INTERNATIONAL
Emerald House
411 University Ridge, Suite B14
Greenville, SC 29601, USA
www.ambassador-international.com

AMBASSADOR BOOKS
The Mount
2 Woodstock Link
Belfast, BT6 8DD, Northern Ireland, UK
www.ambassador-international.com

The colophon is a trademark of Ambassador

TO MY MOTHER,

who loves all four-legged creatures.

I was born early one spring morning on a raspberry farm at the foot of the Blue Ridge Mountains. My mama fed me her warm milk and helped me stand up.

My mistress put Mama and me in a homey stall and named me Drupelet. A "drupelet" is one of the tiny juice-filled bumps on a raspberry that together with many others make a raspberry good to eat.

Many humans came to welcome me into the world, just as they would with any new baby. Next to my stall, there were chickens and goats and rows and rows of raspberry vines. I was such a happy little donkey that I would run and jump and kick up my hind legs to express my joy.

One summer afternoon, Mama and I were eating grass way down at the far end of the pasture where I had not been before. When I looked across the meadow, I saw the most beautiful creatures that I could have ever imagined. Their glossy coats shone in the sun, and their legs were long and slender.

Mama explained, "Those are horses." I wanted to invite them to play, but Mama said, "They are expensive, purebred racing horses, Drupelet. They are very special and would never be allowed to play with a common donkey like you."

I walked back to my stall feeling confused. If I was just an unimportant, common donkey, why did people come to see me? Why was my mistress so nice to me? Mama had always been right before, but this time I thought surely she was wrong.

Maybe Wee Tog, the goat, would have a different opinion. When I explained the situation, he looked at me sympathetically and shook his head sadly.

"I know it hurts your feelings, Drupelet, but your mama is right. You are just a farm animal like the rest of us. Think about your name. You are named after something that is only a part of a raspberry. So go on and play with the other animals and quit moping around."

Throughout the fall, I spent many lonely afternoons at the far end of the pasture, gazing over at the racehorses. I longed to be their friend. I wished I could run as fast and look as beautiful as they did.

At the beginning of winter, a truck arrived at our farm pulling a metal trailer. The driver had a friendly conversation with my mistress, who then led me to the trailer. I was scared and tried to run away. My mistress stroked me gently and talked softly to me until finally I was inside. I heard my mama braying to me, "Drupelet, don't be afraid!"

As I traveled along on the short trip in the trailer, I saw wondrous sights. Houses sparkled with red, green, and white lights. Tall pines were wrapped in garlands of glowing colors.

When the driver stopped and led me out of the trailer, I was greeted happily by sheep, goats, and even three camels. I expected to see the racehorses at this grand event, but there wasn't a single one anywhere.

Everything was strange. The humans were dressed in heavy, drab garments that looked like the sacks my oats came in. There was a baby human that they wrapped in blankets. Then, strangest of all, they placed the baby human in a manger filled with soft hay.

For hours on that crisp, cold evening, groups of people came and quietly watched us. My job was to stay still. Occasionally, the young human girl would sit softly on my back. I had a mixture of feelings, both pride and humility, to be near her and to be part of this mysterious scene.

By the time the driver loaded me gently back onto the trailer, my head and my heart were full of wonder at this strange and unexpected evening. I felt important and special but I didn't know why. The next morning, I told Mama and my raspberry farm friends all about my adventure.

*B*uster, the wise old barn cat, listened to my story especially carefully. He said, "Once I happened upon this same event at a time that the humans call 'Christmas.' Drupelet, you were part of a nativity scene depicting the birth of Jesus, the Son of God, Who was born in a stable and laid in a manger. God sent Jesus to prepare the way for humans to go to heaven when they die. Last night, Drupelet, you were chosen to be the donkey that Mary, the mother of Jesus, rode into Bethlehem so her baby could be born exactly where the Bible had said He would be born!"

*M*y heart was filled with so much joy that I ran and jumped and kicked up my hind legs just as I used to do in the spring. Now I had confidence in my purpose. Although I'm named after a part of the raspberry, it doesn't mean that I am unimportant. It takes the single drupelet and many others for the fruit to be beautiful and delicious. I shouldn't want to be a racehorse to be important. I should only want to be who I am. I wasn't meant to be a racehorse.

I was meant to be the Christmas donkey!

Every year, at the beginning of winter, the same kind man drives his trailer up to my stall. Every year, I am the Christmas donkey that reminds people that Mary, the mother of Jesus, was carried to His birthplace on the back of a common donkey just like me.

DRUPELET

MAMA

BUSTER

WEE TOG

About the Author

Through many years of bedtime stories with her sons Robert and Stephen, a love of children's literature was kindled. When the time came they would no longer sit and listen, Donna began to write her own stories. *The Christmas Donkey* was written as a gift to her mother for Mother's Day. She resides in the Upstate of South Carolina with her loving husband, sons, a dog and two cats.

About Our Farm

Mountain View Berry Farm is a working raspberry and blueberry farm nestled in the foothills of the Blue Ridge Mountains near Landrum South Carolina.

The farm is blessed with The Christmas Donkey, Drupelet, who was born on the farm along with Gus her brother and their Mother Candy, two goats, Wee Tog and Amber, cats Buster and Mu Mu, Rojo the dog and many free-range chickens, all providing a peaceful joy for their owners.

1095 S Shamrock Ave
Landrum, SC 29356
Phone: 864-457-6585

About Lynne Ballenger Pryor

As a lifelong South Carolinian, Lynne has called the upstate her home. This is Lynne's first illustrated book and she is delightfully excited about *The Christmas Donkey*. It was a welcoming experience and excellent therapy to be a part of the book during her recent struggle with breast cancer. These illustrations became very theraputic and provided much comfort and laughter for her during a difficult time in life.

Lynne received a BFA in Studio Art with an emphasis in Communications from Columbia College. During her career, Lynne worked with with many companies as a graphic artist. As her love for art grew, watercolors became her main focus. Lynne is a stay-at-home mom who continues to pursue her passion through watercolors. She has several prints available, and enjoys commission work as well.